Tomb of the Blue Demons

The Bronze Sword Cycles, Volume 0.5

JTT Ryder

Published by JTT Ryder, 2022.

This is a work of fiction. Similarities to real people, places, or events are entirely coincidental.

TOMB OF THE BLUE DEMONS

First edition. February 17, 2022.

Copyright © 2022 JTT Ryder.

ISBN: 979-8215626979

Written by JTT Ryder.

Table of Contents

Prologue

I loved her once, the dragon that she is. I yearn for her now, on the last day of my life. Her constricting grip on me will never be relaxed, even as I face death, and stare deep into the well of the Underworld.

At the twilight of our clan, her stretched neck looms over us. Her wings cast shadows over each glen, each glade, each landing-place. Her glowing, red-yellow eyes never stray from our home.

Slighan, the queen of the Hillmen, has invaded, as she promised to do sixteen years ago. Now her hordes come for us, and our clan Ashaiger is crunched between her teeth.

Once, I had a passion that burned for Slighan, and I slew in her name. Now, while her white neck remains unmarred, I cannot rest, because I know her invasion is the end of our clan.

I now relay all to you with just the two of us in our darkening home. My daughter, Myrnna, your memory is unmatched. You ought to have been a bard if women could become bards. You studied at the druid's academy on Mona, where all druids learn their craft. You were nearly a druidess, and I could never have been prouder of you for it. I don't know what the future holds for you, but I will ensure you have a future in our world of Taman.

I will sacrifice all so that you have a future, but first, I owe you an explanation.

Chapter I

There in the nemeton, the sacred grove to goddess Danu, I sat pondering at midday. At a fissure in a gentle glade, I stared down into its dark depths of Annwyn, the Underworld. These places – caves, rock shelters, crevices – is where our world of Taman and Annwyn met. The sidhe, the beings which haunt everywhere that men ought not to walk, dwell in those places. Many claim to see the sidhe, even confide in them or draw power from them, but never offered proof. As a druid, the highest of the highborn in my clan, I stared down into the blackness of the fissure and asked the gods below to grant me *the sight* – the ability to see the sidhe.

At the crack, I met the Underworld, where we all go when we die, to rest with our ancestors until we are deemed worthy of rebirth on Taman. Did *the sight* really exist? Will *the sight* come to me? Who, if not a druid, would know that?

Daily, I pondered alone in the nemeton, ash-bough staff at my side, birdsongs in my ears, eyes lowered to the Underworld. A week had passed since Beltane, where the title of druid had been bestowed upon me, and I thought I ought to travel before I return home to the isle of Skye. I thought to confer with fellow druids or other learned men, though my betrothed awaited me on my home island, separated from my side for twenty years when I had left for the academy.

Word had gotten to me that some Greeks or Romans sailed to our island earlier in the day, and that one requested to meet me. Eager to meet some more learned men, especially foreigners who wield different knowledge than us druids, I waited there in the grove.

Some footsteps over yonder disturbed the silence of the grove. Between the dense ash boles and under the boughs, my cousin, Vericus, arrived. He had journeyed to the island of Mona after fighting among the mercenaries around Albion. My eyes teared up as he stepped into the sunbeam in the glade.

Vericus, clad in a salmon-coloured cloak over a red-striped white shirt, with baggy check pants hiked up somewhat too high, approached me, sword dangling at his side. He had aged, as did I, the two of us hoary.

'My cousin, Ambicatos,' he said with outstretched arms. 'I can say that I am a warrior, as sure as you can say that you are a druid. I have slain brave men, maimed many more, and routed countless others. I hope you are proud of me.'

'We walked down different paths, yet the Goddess Danu had our feet lead us here today, and our grandfather rests peacefully in the Otherworld,' I said. We spent time in the shade recounting our lives apart. I learned that he had arrived with the Greek ship, and that my friend, Antonius Fabia, a Roman, had been the one who requested my audience.

Stooping under a bough, Antonius, with his frosty stubbled face, emerged from the greenery. He had grey streaks in his curly hair, and a scar crisscrossed his chin. Recently retired from the Roman infantry, he wore a red tunic and brown breeches, and still carried his gladius at his belt. He crossed his veined, corded forearms over his chest and gave us a wry grin.

'Twenty years have flown by like the hoopoe – stolen away,' he said.

'My dear Antonius,' I said, 'it has been so long. You told me you would return, and you have. You have grown older and more handsome.'

'Flattery is always welcome, you know, my friend – but I came here on a Greek ship, and they will soon depart for Italia. I implore you to join me! War is raging in Italia, and soon I may be called to fight again, even in my retirement – the Roman priests wish for you druids to visit Italia, so you may help consult the gods on how to conduct our war. I informed some Etruscans priests about you, and they sent for you – on my word – you are invited to study in Etruria. We can all board the ship at the dock, and venture there straightaway.'

Wordless, I sat there on the stump and climbed to my feet. We embraced, and held each other tight. 'But I am to be betrothed when I return northward to Skye,' I said.

'Just a season!' he said with a laugh, and let me go, 'catch the right wind and with a sacrifice to Uranus, we will be in Etruria in a week. You'll be back before autumn!'

Vericus looked over at me, and he smiled. 'Let me be with you – I will guard you. My sword for your druid's staff! A season of war in Italia ought to make my father proud when I return to him on the isle of Eigg.'

'I suppose it is settled,' I said, 'onward, then, Vericus, Antonius – to Etruria!'

At the dock, Antonius pulled the stopper out of a clay-red amphora that stood waist-high. He, Vericus, and I lifted it and out poured wine into the ocean, its red-brown foaming in the grey sea, serving as a hefty sacrifice to Mannanen, god of sailors, and his Roman cousin, Uranus. Under an overcast sky, we boarded the big Greek trireme. The oarsmen rowed hard to propel the ship out of the harbour. With the sail hoisted and unfurled, we disembarked. And with the west wind in our sail, we journeyed southward.

Mannanen-Uranus blessed us with good weather, and it took us just six days to sail to the Balearics, via Armorica and Iberia. While moored in the Gymnesiai Isles, we heard of the war raging about Italia, Sardinia, and Sicilia. The Romans and the Carthaginians butted heads like two horny bulls on a pasture; they riddled the Italian peninsula in rapine and plunder.

'We will find safe passage to Etruria,' Antonius said, as the ship rocked in the ebb, 'we will avoid the battles if we can, but I fear that Mars will hoist us up onto his fields.'

'Aye, if Camulus, Mars' cousin, decides,' Vericus said with a grin and a hand on his sword's antler-covered handle. Some slaves, knee-deep in the sea below, scraped the last of the barnacles off the ship.

'I've heard that Etruscans have a peculiar view of the Underworld,' I said to Antonius, 'and I am determined to learn from them, war or not.'

'My dear friend,' Antonius said as he swallowed, 'there is someone who is nosing around Etruria doing just that, questioning the Etruscan priests, and prodding about the old tombs. I suggest you stay away from her.'

The gulf of the ocean in my sight, I lifted my head into the breeze, and wondered what woman could invoke such a warning from Antonius. Then, the ship's captain ordered the last of the men onto the ship. After boarding, the oarsmen all settled on the benches and readied their oars.

I must say, my daughter, that his warning did nothing but blow the bellows of my curiosity.

Chapter II

We arrived in the port of Tarquinia the following morning and headed to the city and, my daughter, I will tell you that I had never seen anything so glorious. The wonders spun around me like the cinders of a burning wheel. Entire sculptures of the likeness of men reposing. Tall buildings of cut worked stone. Blue and yellow temples along roads paved in cobblestones, flanked by rearing life-sized, bronze horses. All these wonders I could never recount in full, and I urge you, my daughter, to see the glory of the South at least once in your life.

The Romans had set up what they called a colony in the area, and they took tribute from the Etruscans, particularly their women who were tasked to weave sailcloth for the Romans. All the meanwhile, gruff, tired, and broken men passed through the city, the war raging in the lush fields of Campania to the far south, springing up deserters and traitors like polecats spring out hares from holes.

Word quickly spread around the city that a druid from the far north had arrived. We spent many afternoons in the olive tree groves in conversation. I knew nothing of the Etruscan language, though my Latin allowed me to converse. We spoke of the stars, of deep philosophy. All the while I learned about just how large Taman is, and of countless men and their mores. My overall interest, however, lay with the Etruscan view of the dead, and their Underworld.

Antonius, to add wax to my candle, arranged a tour to the necropolis of Etruria. We embarked at dawn, with companions of Antonius and their slaves, and travelled by cart. We arrived at the necropolis at midmorning, with the sun beating down, the seemingly endless avenues like so many uncoiled snakes.

The dead had been interred in crofts in the tufa hillocks, where countless tombs had been hollowed out for hundreds of years. Inside the tombs, beds had been carved from the tufa, where many of the skeletal dead still lay, adorned with spears or swords, or gold goblets, or pots half the size of a man, or with heaps of bones from funerary feasts, or other precious possessions, all left unscarred and in place by the dutiful custodians of their descendants. Others dead lay in sarcophagi, some with lids of carved marble in the likeness of the deceased. These were halls of the ancestors of the Etruscans, and their descendants tended to them.

We walked from tomb to tomb and discussed much about the augury of the Etruscans. Like us, they rely on the flights of birds, and the patterns of the entrails of a sow or ewe or heifer spilt out under the knife on the altar, to understand the ways of the Gods.

Antonius led us to one tomb, which he informed us possessed a chair hewn from stone. The chair, he said, was where descendants would sit and wait in honour of the ancestors, as if waiting their turn for death. My friend entered the tomb first, and in mid-sentence, gasped. We hurried in, only to find that there was someone seated on the stone chair.

A woman was sitting still on the chair, her eyes closed, and with the soles of her sandaled feet touching one another. She paid us no mind. Antonius muttered in Latin, turned to us and began his speech.

The damp air of the dark tomb cooled me as Antonius spoke about the glories of the ancestral seat, as if the woman had not been sitting there. After he had finished, his companions left the tomb. He grabbed my arm, and pulled me toward the sunny portico. As I followed him, the woman opened her dark eyes, and she winked at me.

Outside, the sun blazed hot, and I swiped a spider off my shoulder. We sat on blankets over the burnished gravel road that sprawled throughout the necropolis. The slave girls, two Teuton lasses, served us fried dormice and jars of honey from the cart. I grabbed a dormouse by the bare tail, dipped it into the honey, and sucked the meat off its bones. Antonius grabbed me by the arm, and spoke in a low tone.

'She was not supposed to be sitting there. No one is permitted to sit there, save for the children of the deceased!'

'Why doesn't anyone banish her, then? Send her off on her way?'

'I would like to think our Etruscan friends are too busy whining about the Romans to concern themselves with her, but in truth, many of the locals, well, they fear her,' he said in a lowered voice. 'She is a mystery around Italia. They call her one of the three sorceresses.'

I sat baffled, grizzled dormouse twixt my fingers.

'Another title for her is *the Armenian*,' he said, 'but I don't know if she is from Armenia. No one knows where she calls home. No one knows her age. No one knows her name.'

He lowered his voice even more. 'They fear her because she has been rumoured to be assembling deserters from the war. We cannot prove it yet,' he ceased talking.

'Antonius Fabia! Shall you not introduce me to your companion?' a sultry voice said from behind me in *Gaulish*. I looked over my shoulder. Out from the entrance of the tomb came *the Armenian*. She wore a long, fringed thin yellow wool cloak. Her long raven-black hair was unbound, capped with a linen bonnet. She had milky skin, red lips, and the darkest, blackest eyes I had ever seen. Her nose was long and regal, her eyebrows were two black arcs, her breasts round behind the veneer of her pure white linen dress. Her toes, sandaled, danced.

'Why, Antonius Fabia, you were just discussing me with your friend.'

'You were in prayer, didn't want to bother you,' Antonius said with a wry grin.

'Why didn't you inform me you had a druid with you? And a Briton, nonetheless?' she said, and a gentle hand touched my shoulder.

One slave girl hastily ransacked through a bag and pulled out another blanket, while another approached her with a platter of honey-fried dormice.

She held out a hand, smiling. 'No, thank you,' she said in the language of the Teutons. Her dark eyes turned to me, and she spoke in my tongue, and with a wide grin, she said 'I would much rather go for a stroll – won't you grace me with your presence?'

Our eyes locked. 'Don't you want to speak to someone who can speak Briton?'

Antonius grabbed me by the hand. 'Don't believe a venomous word that spits from that forked-tongue.'

Her hand pressed down on my shoulder, and when she leaned her head over me, her perfume smelled delightful. 'Ah – you have such a way with words, Antonius Fabia! Shall you be an orator, shall you march into the Curia down in Rome – and tell them all about me, then? Dazzle them with your great speeches! Rouse them to violence! Soldiers shall fly from all fields and fight for you and apprehend me! Why – you do say a lot of words, but nothing ever seems to happen after!'

'My good Antonius,' I said to him, 'I know you trust my judgment.'

'Beware her tongue,' he said, his eyes sombre, as he released my hand. *The Armenian* took my hand, her softness against my callouses, her perfume smelling like a bundle of flowers.

She stuck her tongue out. 'Do you see a split?' she asked, muffled, her eyes aflutter in glee. She slurped her tongue back in, then asked the slave girls something in Teutonic. They brought over a vat of olive oil. A few paces from us, she unhooked her cloak, and unstrapped her dress. Two slave girls went over and oiled her toned shoulders, across her straight neck, up and down her long legs, her white skin becoming shinier in the sunlight. I swallowed as she threw her head back and raised her arms in the air, her lithe body bent.

Vericus shrugged. 'Just call my name, cousin,' he said, hand on his hilt, 'and as sure as Cuchulainn stood against his enemies, my sword is your shield, by Camulus!'

I nodded, and Antonius grasped my arm.

'Not by Camulus, but by Eros, she will have you like a weasel has eggs in a motherless nest,' Antonius said.

The woman thanked the slave girls, dressed, and stuck her tongue out again at Antonius. She approached me, her hips swaying, and leaned up against my sweaty body. Her slimy arm wrapped around mine, and pulled me away from the crowd.

We strolled down an avenue in the Etruscan necropolis, the porticos of shadowy tombs gaping on either side of us. Birds chirped from the green canopy. We rounded a corner, and I finally found something to say.

'How do you know my language? Many men can speak Gaulish to me – only it is what they speak in Cisalpine Gaul – but you, you may as well be from Skye.'

'I knew a druid from there once,' she said, 'he was very old, thus he walks Gaia no more, but methinks his shade guides me. And he's guided me to you.'

'What was his name?'

'I prefer not to reveal it. I would not want you to curse him, if you were to regret meeting me,' she said, her head bowed a bit.

We stopped and her dark eyes met mine.

'What is your name?'

'Ambicatos,' I said.

'Ambicatos! He-who-fights-from-all sides! The name of a legend! You must fight like him!'

'Perhaps, but I am a fighter no longer...' I said.

'Are you not?' she said, and ran a finger down my shoulder. She half-grinned as she crested the height of my muscle. 'You are always a fighter if it is in your blood. Even a man who has never trained to be a warrior can fight, even in his old age, if the right cause arises.'

'Then let me fight again before I am frail,' I said. 'But what is your name?'

'Slighan,' she said, and grinned.

'Now, that name sounds exactly like the name of a mountain on Skye, we call it the Slighan Hill.'

'Oh, is it? Tell me more,' she said and grinned wider.

'It means a shelly place. Why a mountain would be named that is unknown, as is why a woman would be called such. Especially an outlander, as you are. Rather, you can tell me more.'

'I asked first,' she said, as she grabbed my hand and walked me further down the avenue. After scaling a hill, we walked seaward. The Tyrrhenian brine-breeze cooled me. 'Did a Briton druid come all the way to Italia to be silent about his wisdom?'

'It's a prominent mountain,' I said, 'reddish. Crowned in a cairn from elder times. Locals believe the Cailleach, our goddess of winter, resides there. They even tell their children to beware the *hag of the hills*, if they are around the foothills grazing their sheep and cattle.'

'Now, Ambicatos, tell me, why do you think I, a so-called sorceress, would be so interested in a mountain on your home island?'

'Perhaps you're interested in sacred mountains – where the gods and man can meet.'

'Are the druids not that? Why else would you spend twenty years on Mona, if not to be the bridge between man and the divine?'

'In the groves, in deep caves, on mountain peaks, we meet the gods more easily.'

'Yes, indeed. And why would I be called after a mountain?'

I said nothing. She placed a soft hand on my face, and drew closer to me. I took a breath. She stood nearly as tall as I, tall for a woman, and her dress danced against my white robe. 'I will take you across the bridge.'

'A sorceress,' I said, 'tell me, what does that mean?'

'It means you men don't understand me,' she said, and she turned her face to giggle. 'You spend your lives studying from masters, yet who teaches the masters?

'I will teach you. I will show how little you know, and how much I know. Now, return to your little group of men, waited on by little girls, eating the cuisine of their conquerors! Discuss what you learned from the self-fancied masters! Do it while men are hung from olive tree groves to ensure victory against their enemies. Do it while women scream, are stripped, and raped. Do it while children bury their fathers and coo on their mother's ravished bosoms! Do it while the Etruscans pay the Romans in silver, slaves, and sailcloth – your hosts to their masters!

'I will be here, dancing from one world to the other. In Tarquinia, at dawn tomorrow, we meet outside the hostel, and journey to the Underworld together. Then, you learn!'

She leaned in, her lips brushed against mine, and she wiped a globule of olive oil across my face, and she twirled away. She swayed down the avenue amidst the tombs, and vanished in the gloominess of the distance. I headed back toward Antonius and his group, sat in silence and drank my wine and ate my dormice.

My dear daughter, what I shall relay to you next is something for your ears alone. If the guilt of the burden weighs too heavily on you, you may relieve it to your dearest betrothed. What I will relay is perhaps to you unbelievable, but I assure you, the Gods left me bereft of disbelief. I relay to you what happened between me and *the Armenian*, or the sorceress... or as she is known to her legions now: Queen Slighan.

Chapter III

Vericus had joined me, armed as always, the breeze blowing through his greying, spiky hair. Antonius had opted to stay among his friends back in Tarquinia. While eating grapes in the shade of the olive tree near the road, a two-horse carriage pulled up to us on the road outside the city. It was driven by a drab-dressed, dark-haired, bearded man. Slighan climbed down, and her handmaidens followed. Her handmaidens had dark hair and dark eyes, which was not odd for Italia, but I noticed an odd sheen in the hair of a girl about fifteen Samhains who drove Slighan's wagon.

The cart carried on over the paved road, the cartwheels firmly in the ruts of the stones. We travelled downriver, and once we came to the uplands, from the hills we saw patchworks of farms sprawled out, abounding the valleys. Mist clung to the hills like babes at breasts in the early morning, and by the time afternoon struck, it had all become sunny and the mist had faded. We took a break, lay in the shade, and the servants washed and fed us.

I slept until something tugged on my arm. I awoke and Slighan had grabbed my arm in both of her hands, pulling me up like a child awakening their parent.

'Let me show you something,' she said through a muffled giggle, 'while they are all asleep.'

She led me into a nearby olive grove, where her things had been splayed out on a blanket underneath the shade. She cantered over, beckoned me to follow, and from a wicker basket she pulled out a small bone-constructed box. She pulled the lid off, flipped it, and placed a small figure on its underside. She brandished it at me.

I had never seen something as strange as it before. It was a woman's figure, an old woman, fat, perhaps from pregnancy or age. It was headless, and the backside was bare, whereas most of the detail of the work had gone into the breasts and the vulva, both stark and puffy. I knew that both the Greeks and Romans alike shunned away from displaying the vulva of a woman, and my own people rarely carved images of men besides their faces.

'This is old,' she said, her eyes slits, her grin wide, and she bowed her head. 'Older than Rome. Older than Homer. Older than the cairn of the Slighan Hill. Older than all.'

Such a thing, I reckoned, would have been banished if an order of druids got a hold of it. It looked otherworldly; not for the eyes of the men of Taman. It was perhaps from the sidhe, and such things could have brought us ill luck.

'You are scared,' she said. She grabbed my hand and stifled my tremors. 'You should be.'

'It's of the sidhe – what was it carved from?' I said, and rose, but she gripped my hand hard, and I went back down.

'A circus master claimed it is elephant tusk, as did a Carthaginian merchant, but no one knows what image it is, truly. Not the southernmost Ethiopian, the northernmost Finn, the westernmost Briton, or the Easternmost Indian. It is beyond this world.'

'Why do you have it?'

'It brings me dreams,' she said, 'this is a goddess, a long, old, forgotten goddess. I have such long, vivid, lucid, luscious, succulent, darling dreams when I sleep with her under my pillow. Oh!'

An urge for me to take myself away struck me, harder than hunger. I slipped out of her grasp.

'A student of Druidry fears suchlike?' she asked, and she rose and stood on her tiptoes. 'The druids, the most knowledgeable men on Gaia, the ones who walk the twilight betwixt this world and the Otherworld – shirks, dreads, and fears such a goddess? Methinks something is afoot! Methinks, perchance, this goddess shines truth, and that you, Ambicatos, fear truth.'

'I fear nothing but the world coming out from under me and the sky falling onto me.'

She laughed. 'Said the Gaul to Alexander! A warrior's mantra, is that what you defend yourself with?'

'If I am faced with such evil, then perhaps I will walk as a warrior again.'

'The hero of your people, Cuchulainn, who dared to face his enemies on his own two feet, the Morrigan in the guise of a crow on his shoulder – what Gaul who knows that story bows down to the empire? That is why the Romans and Carthaginians alike adore you Gauls as auxiliaries! When red Mars rouses man, when the ecstasy of battle descends like the eagle, the face of the Gaul warps, the warp-spasm, which Cuchulainn had. Ah, to be in the arms of a brave Gaul...

'Enough distractions,' she said and smiled, and she twirled in the yellow grass, and then she tiptoed toward me, her light linen dress ruffling in the wind against her legs. 'The dreams! Tell me, what do you Britons say about the world? How was it formed, and what happened when it had been made so?'

'Our ancestors travelled westward, and slew the giants that lived in our islands, to make room for us.'

She grinned wider. 'Yes – giants! There were giants, always giants, always to be slain and to make room for your ancestors. Do you know what I dreamt?'

I said nothing, as she grabbed hold of my wrist and pulled me into the shade of another olive tree. I glanced over my shoulder to see the little statuette still there.

'I dreamt of a reddish hill, topped by a cairn of elder times. There, upon the cairn, a dragon resided. A red dragon, with the wingspan of ninety-nine eagles, with the neck the size of nine-hundred snakes, and fire-breath nine-thousand tongues of flame. And there I saw myself, upon that hill, and when I looked into the dragon's eyes, I saw legions of men marching, with stone-bladed weapons, in dark clothing, with black-dyed hair, giants they were, and they marched to the tune of my voice.

'Then I became learned. They were no giants, but men, and they had been slaughtered by your ancestors,' she lowered her voice. 'They were men. Not just men, but women, and children, animals. They lived on farms. They had simple lives. They knapped their tools from stone – from flint, from quartz, from shale. They lived happily. Then, from the east, came men baring bronze. Bronze swords. Bronze spears. Bronze daggers. They came in waves; each wave crashed and drove the originals – the First Men – away. They made room, as you said. The statuettes of the goddess were crafted no more.

'The Slighan Hill,' she said, 'your goddess, the Cailleach, leads me there in my dreams. I know there, on that mountain, is my destiny.'

'You're breathing heavy,' she said, once again smiling, but her eyes looked wet. I had been drawn back toward the tree, stuck to it as if the bark had been glued. She pursued me, and leaned her head against my shoulder.

'That is what I dreamt,' she said, 'that is what I am dreaming. That is what dreams yet to come shall be. I know,' she said, locking eyes with me. 'I know. I know more than the priests of Rome, or Egypt, or Babylon, or even India and yet further still, Serica! No one but I, but I, the so-called *Armenian*, one of three sorceresses, know.'

'This is against all I learned,' I said.

'Ah, but it is not. Tell me, then, fletching druid, what have the gods passed down to you? What have they taught you? Whom did your ancestors slay, and from where did they come from?'

'Giants and we came from the east. But it was so long ago, so dim, dimmer than the times when we had our mummies in our walls, murkier than when we had not yet known iron, and foggier than before the Romans arrived from Troy. You dream, but how do you know it is the truth?'

'The truth will be revealed on the morrow,' she said and slunk away. 'On with your nap, budding druid.'

Slighan nestled around with her things, giving low orders to her servants, and then huddled against me. In the shade of the olive tree, we laid reclined on a blanket, my hands folded over my chest, her head on my shoulder. A handmaiden brought a rosy silk-covered pillow for her head, and she said nothing as her breathing became heavier. I closed my eyes and my breathing followed hers, but at one point, she stirred, awoke, and patted the circlet of hair around my shaven scalp.

'You think you know, because of your tonsure,' she whispered. 'Sleep, little druid. I will show you everything in the tomb.'

After a spell, she fell asleep. Her handmaidens gathered in the grove with some stones, and they formed a campfire. There were nine of them, all dark-haired, dressed in drab wool that looked matte against their bronzed, oiled skin. Some fetched wood in a train, while others spread the kindle from a tinderbox in the ring of stones. One girl, the eldest, armed herself with flint and iron, and sparked some flames. Vericus approached them, extending his hand to help, but the girls shooed him away. He walked away, leaned against a tree nine paces away from us, and rested there in the shade.

Another girl, of around sixteen Samhains, came up from the river with a bucket and hung it from an iron tripod over the fire. Two other handmaidens came back with a vat and placed it down in between themselves. They had grey handprints all over themselves – including on their breasts and buttocks – as though they were youth playing in mud. Each girl stood over the bucket, and one by one, took out a clump of something. Through my peering eyes, I could see they had grey-blue stuffs, probably clay. They squatted around the vat, rolling the clay on the ground, shaping it, while the eldest girl directed them. As the water behind them broiled, one of the girls held up a clay figure. It looked like that ivory headless woman, standing knee-height.

Each of the girls had a clay headless woman apiece, and they held them aloft their heads. They circled the fire, and each one smashed the clay figure against the fire ring around the campfire. The figure was splattered each time, and as they did that, the eldest girl, armed with a shovel, fed ash from the fire into the bucket, while another cracked eggs. Once each clay figure had been smashed, the girls ducked their heads into the bucket one by one. When they lifted their wet heads, their hair looked darker and shinier. With seashell combs, they combed each other's wet hair, humming lowly. Slighan slept silently throughout it.

The eldest girl removed the steaming cauldron from the fire, and setting it aside, re-joined the circle. The nine girls gripped each other's wrists and ran around the fire. The flames danced at the wind they created, their encirclement dizzying, and I nearly forgot to feign sleep. After a long spell of spinning, the girls all let their hands go. One of the girls slipped in the ashy grass, and her body bent the blaze of the fire. She caught herself like an acrobat, her lithe body hanging backwards in the smoke. Her sisters pulled her up, and she flopped her shiny, black hair in front of her, its edges all singed. They spread charcoal over their faces around the smoky campfire, giggling. All nine ashy-faced, black-haired, clay-clad girls backed away from the fire, and then ran off toward the river. With their garments flung through the air and around the riverbank, they all dove naked into the water.

I glanced over at Vericus, who raised an eyebrow, shrugged, and with a grin headed riverward. I leaned my head back against the olive tree trunk and fell asleep.

Chapter IV

'Before we go to the tombs, I will show you,' Slighan said, as she shook me awake. 'Get up, wash your face. It is just an hour's journey from here. We will eat on the way.'

We traversed through the rolling green hills, toward the Apennines, through the wineries, and around the forests that skirt the mountains. We moved up toward what looked like an old mineshaft. It was a black gap in the side of the cliff, child-sized. Leaving Vericus and the handmaidens at the base of the hill, we scrambled up the steep slope toward the open shaft.

'The spirits of the land are harmed when we mine,' she said, pointing at the shaft. 'Rome ought to mine silver elsewhere, for it mines too much in Etruria. The spirits groan and moan and whimper with each crack of the mattock. This one is abandoned, yet the spirits are astir. Do you hear anything?'

I put my ear to the mineshaft. An echo, a faint drop, the long gulf yawned back at me much like a seashell. Nothing, however, seemed abnormal.

'No.'

She pushed me gently aside, and, closing her eyes, she put her ear to the shaft. Now, my daughter, you know very well what could happen when someone with *the sight* is in your presence. Even if you do not possess it yourself, the world warps like the face of Cuchulainn.

'The spirits robbed of their silver cry out,' she said. 'Do you not hear them?'

A low moan, scratchy and chain-like, emitted from the shaft. Slighan eyed me, while all-around had become darker, as if day had faded into the night without twilight. After a few heartbeats, another groan crawled out from the shaft.

'This is a shaft without silver. There is no glint, no shine, no sheen. Nothing but dullness, dryness, darkness. Yet you can see them.'

Two of her handmaidens produced a torch, and with a flick of iron against flint, the torch was alight and illuminated the shaft.

Something deep in the red-yellow darkness moved, a glimpse of a being. I blinked and averted my gaze, back to Slighan, whose face looked askew in the dancing light.

'Why did you look away?' she said, now askance.

'There are some things men of Taman should not see,' I said.

'You amaze me,' she said, wiping her brow, 'you are not afraid, you just respect them.'

'I know what I will see, and I should not see it. I think the spirits here should be left to rest, and not be disturbed by my gawking,' I said, but the truth was, my daughter, I tired of showing her my weakness.

'But do you now understand? The spirits were not here until I called them,' she said, and grinned.

'How could you? After my twenty years in the druid's academy, I thought the sidhe were too far from us. It seemed that just old ladies and children alone could see them.'

'The bridge,' she said, 'I am the bridge. Tell me.' Her face slunk close to mine. 'Do you want to know more?'

Biting my lip, I nodded.

I turned to leave, and, gripping my hand, she pulled me away. 'We shall make haste to Tarquinia. There, a portal to the Underworld lays. I will bridge you to it!'

Chapter V

We travelled westward down the grey road at nightfall, flanked by tall shadows of mountains beyond distant gloomy vineyards. We approached a crossroad where the roads parted like two white branches split. There, some people had gathered around a marble statue of Mercury, the Roman God of travellers. For us, whom the Romans call Gauls or Britons, we worship him as Lugus. Some of our cousins, who have adopted Roman mores, call him Mercury-Lugus.

At the statue, we met a trio of men. They called out to us in the Gaulish tongue – Slighan called back out. Out of the shadows around the crossroads, dozens of figures emerged. They all dressed darkly, with grey and brown hoods lit by torches.

'Don't be alarmed, my dear druid,' Slighan said, 'you have just met the new dawn in the dark!'

A leader, I assumed, among the newcomers approached. In the torchlight, he looked gruff and hard, with a sunburnt face. He had a thick moustache, but stubble had grown out around his face, as a budding beard. He spoke in Gaulish, a thick accent for me, but the tongue was similar enough to mine, so I followed them.

'There are thirty-six of us,' he said, the red-yellow torchlight gleaming in his eyes. 'Each of us command over ninety-men apiece. Many of us have a brother, a brother-in-law, a son, or a nephew who command several more. We sacrifice at the foot of Mercury-Lugus now for more safe travellers to arrive here, to heed what harbingers of peace such as yourself have to offer.'

There was a white-shirted man in a brown hat, holding a copper vessel. He sprinkled water on the marble feet of Mercury. I went forth, to join the worshippers, but Slighan grabbed me by the shoulder.

'We need not sacrifice to anyone but Hecate,' she said.

'It is uncomfortable,' I said, 'to pass a god and not give thanks.'

'A druid,' the moustached-man said to me, his eyes ablaze as they affixed to my haircut and lowered down to my white robe. 'And Vericus!' he looked over at my cousin, who smiled at him. They grabbed each other's arms.

'It's been a long time since the days we fought alongside one another, Divico,' Vericus said.

'May it not be the last, Vericus,' Divico said. 'Have you sworn loyalty to *the Armenian*?'

'Nay,' Vericus said. Divico pulled back, and his men became astir, grasping their weapons.

'My old friend and comrade – by Camulus, god of war – do not tell me that you have sworn fealty to Rome!'

'Ease – peace – Divico,' Slighan said before Vericus could respond, 'he has neither loyalty to the Romans nor the Carthaginians – no need to redden, battle-mad Gaul. Nay – redden – blacken even – hold it dearly and let it foment, a bubbling cauldron within you! Soon you shall overflow, and scorch the feet of all those who have wronged us.

'Now it begins,' she said, as she climbed up on the wagon, and gestured down around her handmaidens.

'Good lady,' said the Gaul, 'both the Romans and Carthaginians have scouts and spies. Should we linger here too long, we risk being spotted.'

'Yet bravery flows in me!' she shouted, 'let them come. What good would they be, tired and beaten as they are, against your weapons, if you are so passioned?'

The thirty-six men around the crossroads roused, muttering to themselves, looking to and fro.

'By Hecate – swear to me!' Slighan said. 'Your oaths, and you will be my oathsmen. We are not new to this world – we are the First Men, and First Men we all shall be! Now, witness the Otherworld that you should fear.'

Slighan's handmaidens, all black-haired, came forward and they all danced around the wagon. Slighan wiggled her arms, and the light around us darkened. At first, I thought a torch had gone out, but then the Gauls around me all gasped. One implored another to look up at the sky, and I followed his gaze. A shadow passed over the moon, and little red eyes glowed in the darkness, flanking the crossroads from both sides.

'Who can promise you this? Your priests at Moloch's fire? Your Flamens who hold the knife to the sheep's throat? Could your mathematicians calculate what happened there? Even the Egyptian magicians have never produced such a sight to behold!

'And what say you, druid?' she asked me.

'An omen, for certain,' I said with a heavy sigh.

She pointed a finger at the Gauls. 'Swear an oath to me – and fight for me – the gods have commanded it! Swear an oath to Queen Slighan!'

Slighan stepped off the wagon. One of her handmaidens came forward holding a sceptre of polished greenstone. She called forward the moustached-man, the old Gaul Divico, who removed his hood to reveal a head of beeswaxed-spiked, lime-dyed hair.

Divico approached Slighan, who raised her sceptre to his face. He kissed it.

'On your knees,' she said.

'You'd have to break my knees to get me down on them, especially in front of valorous men, like Vericus,' he said.

A handmaiden stood aghast, and there were some mutterings in the crowd of Gauls. Slighan waited stone-faced for a spell, and then laughed.

'This one has courage,' she said. 'The rest of you ought to know that. Do not think me a tyrant – come forward on your feet, warrior. I just ask that you stoop down since you stand taller than I.'

Divico went forward, and she lifted the sceptre to his face. He kissed it.

'I swear an oath to fight for you, queen Slighan,' he said, and moved to the side.

Now, one by one, they came forward. I knew them now as warriors, probably chiefs, descendants of the god Lugus. They hailed from

Transalpine Gaul; why they were in Italia, I did not know. I could only ascertain that they came over with the Carthaginians, or the Romans employed them as auxiliaries. After each had kissed the sceptre, a handmaiden took them to the side, where they had a vat filled to the brim with a mix of ash and yolk. The handmaidens first washed the wax out of the hair of the Gauls, then had them bow their wet hair into the vat, and they all came up black-headed. Soon, each of the warriors had become oath-sworn and black-haired.

'Now that I have your oaths, arm yourselves with your weapons!'

The handmaidens unveiled the cart, and there laid an array of weapons. In the moonlight, each warrior took a weapon: a spear, an axe, or a mace. Each weapon, however, was made of stone. That is, each spear had a flint-bladed spearhead, and each axe and mace had a stone head attached to wooden hafts. I had only seen the blades and heads of such weapons from the sidhe – they pop up when we plough the fields, or are found in caves or old tombs.

Slighan conversed with her warriors around a campfire offroad, while I waited with Vericus at the foot of the statue of Mercury. I prayed to Mercury-Lugus for safekeeping, well-being, and health on my journey. I sprinkled a little olive oil I had in a flask at his feet. Vericus hummed an old rhyme that our grandmother, Myrnna, sang to us when we were children, and we waited near the shrine until the last candles were snuffed out, and Slighan came back with her retinue of men.

'Some of the men come with us, while the rest have other plans,' she said, and nine men detached themselves from the horde. 'We will get to our destination as promised – by daybreak.'

We passed the statue of Mercury, and taking a deep breath, I climbed onto the wagon. Next to Slighan, we journeyed westward.

Chapter VI

Rosy-fingered dawn rosed the sky as we arrived upon the great hills in the countryside of Tarquinia. We ventured toward the largest hill, yellow with weeds and decked in the scrub. We passed a vineyard, where we spied a boy peering out at us from some dense vines. Up in the hills, we passed grazing sheep, and a sheepdog barked at us. After a span, we reached the top of the hill, where hundreds of tall earth-mounds stood like so many anthills. Some mounds were several men high, and as wide and broad as houses. They were the tombs of esteemed families that forever left their mark upon Taman.

'Gaia is pregnant with the dead,' Slighan said, leaning on my shoulder, 'but there is more to her womb than children.'

We disembarked from the wagon. Slighan's eldest handmaiden handed her a bundle of cypress sprigs, and reprieved herself of her duties.

Slighan ordered her warriors to guard the top of the hill. Appearing as a white ghost among the dark mounds, a man in a bleached white tunic, fringed with scarlet, and a brown cloak dripping in dew came forward.

The man spoke to Slighan in the Etruscan language. He pointed seaward, and repeated the word 'tribunes', a word referring to the military chiefs of the Roman army. Slighan stood awash in pity, her lips puckered, and then she said 'no'. The Etruscan launched down onto his knees, and hugged her knees, his head against her loins. She ran a red-nailed finger through his curly brown hair, then slapped him lightly in the face and laughed.

Two burly, shirtless Gauls in baggy brown trousers, now her bodyguards, hauled the Etruscan up and lugged him away, snarling under their thick, bushy moustaches. Slighan approached me, shading her face with her hand as she walked toward the rising sun over the distant Apennines.

'What a fool that Etruscan priest is – he begged us not to go down into the tombs, because a raven flew southward. Nevermind him – come, I will show you now,' she said.

'Leave us,' she said to her bodyguards and handmaidens. Leaving my cousin Vericus, who raised his other eyebrow this time, Slighan whisked me away.

By the hand, Slighan led me through the avenues of the tombs. Each of the mounds possessed a dark entrance, about man-high. We came toward one mound, where a little light flickered from deep beyond its portico. The entrance was fenced off with some wooden staves. Slighan huffed, and ripped one stave out of the ground and chucked it aside, and the fence bowed over.

'Superstitious! What do they truly know?'

'What was that light down there?' I asked her.

'I did not see it,' she said with a grin, 'perhaps you have a bit of *the sight* yourself? Or perhaps I did see it – listen!'

We stood silent for a spell, and before I could protest, she shushed me. She wrapped her arms around my neck, and hung there for a while. The breeze, a distant donkey bleating, the pleads of the Etruscan priest beyond the mounds all swirled away from me. I heard nothing but her soft breathing, smelled nothing but her lavender perfume, felt nothing but her curvaceous hips, and finally, tasted her carmine lipstick. I flushed, and I meant to inform her that I am betrothed, but then something came up from the chamber of the tomb.

Laughter edged out of the mound, and the sound of metal clinking followed.

'The druid is surprised,' she said, as she smiled. 'Did you mistake my power for mere trickery when I awed those Gauls? Come.'

I lowered my head to enter the tomb. My hands groped the cold dirt walls as I headed down into the mound, following the white blur of Slighan several paces ahead. Mid-entrance, something furry slunk along my ankle, and I looked down to see a mouse scurry away. After a long descent down into the tomb, too long for such a small mound, the spat of laughter resounded from down below. Then there was a light, and I came into it.

A party lay sprawled out before me. There were several men and women, some splayed out on their sides, sipping from silver goblets. Half-dressed slave boys busybodied around, to and fro, re-filling glasses or replenishing plates of grapes. The aroma of boar, and wine, and honey, all came forth. A youthful, topless lady reclined on a bench, spinning a fig between her fingers. She laid a hand down at her side, and some beast rose. It looked like a cat, dog-sized, tawny with black spots. Its eyes, like yellow topazes, glinted in the fire. I would later learn that it was a leopard. It had not noticed me. Someone unseen strummed a lyre.

Dizzied, I gazed around. I walked past a table with a boy chopping a hock of roasted boar. A man, dressed in a long white tunic fringed in red, much like the priest outside, handed the boy a tusk, who took it in his greasy fingers. I waved, to get their attention, but neither responded. I headed over to two women, laughter in their voices, wine in their cups, their breasts bare. They had not seen me. Neither the partyers, nor the slaves, nor the two dog-sized cats noticed me. Slave boys walked past. A boy in a white tunic had been the lyre player, but when he looked at me, he just looked through me. Then I saw his eyes.

Nothing. He had pits for eyes, dark, with a hint of green. I turned to flee, and found a red door behind me. I grabbed the doorknob, and a woman shouted 'No!' as I did. I swung the door open and rushed out. By the time I understood I was not running upward toward the open air, but downward, I found myself in another chamber of the tomb.

In the blackness, I heard unseen water gently lapping at a bank. After a spell, the river rushed out through the chamber. I clambered around to avoid it, but found only a craggy, cold solid tufa wall. A single beam of light spilt out from an unseen oculus and tinted the river silver. The chamber had grown larger, the river was a span across, and from the south came a whistle and the sound of a paddle coming toward me.

Then I erred hard, my daughter. Instead of shirking from the sight that came, I stood and watched. A boat came downriver, from the south. The steerer of the boat was clad in a greasy girdle from which rags hung. He had a long, unkempt beard, and his eyes glowed like the blue of flames. He paddled with one oar, and the boat slowed as it approached me, beaching against the riverbank.

'Have you paid the toll?' he asked. His voice rang like iron.

'I sacrificed to Mercury-Lugus today,' I said, as I headed riverward, through the moist bank, and climbed into the small boat. The ferryman, who smelled like poppies, paddled me across the quiet river. The boat floated across the river as if it skimmed across the creamiest milk, until its stern hit the bank.

'Off you go, and safe travels,' he said. I stepped off, pushed the boat back into the river for him, and found a woman in white waiting for me.

'You daring druid you!' Slighan said with a grin as she grabbed both of my hands. 'Don't you know what you just did?'

'I do,' I said, 'I trust in Mercury-Lugus to protect me, as I am a traveller.'

She laughed. 'The god of travellers is not needed for your egress, fledgling druid! But how pious you are to the gods. Yet you only needed to ask me if you wanted to see the other side.

'I am the bridge,' she said, and she held out a cypress sprig to me, 'between this world and the next. That is the power gifted to the three sorceresses. Come, and let me show you.'

She led me up the riverbank, and into a cavern. Water dripped from the ceiling as we entered into a chamber lit by torchlight. There sat two figures, both blue-skinned men. They wore red wool tunics that were cinched by gold brooches at their collars. They had long, black, wiry hair, black beards, and bulbous noses. They sat on a moss-green divan, drinking wine from silver cups.

'You have brought an outsider before us,' said the one on the left.

'Has he much to offer us?' said the one on the right.

'Nay, my friends, he is barely one who sacrificed to Mercury for a chance to know more, to know the Underworld.'

The two fell silent, and sipped from their cups.

'You,' said Slighan to the blue-skinned men, 'the demons of knowledge, have revealed so much to me. You revealed to me how wrong the so-called philosophers of this world are, how the bards sing dim tales, and how the historians wander helplessly in darker caverns than this. You have taught me much, my dear friends, and I promise that I told no one unworthy of the knowledge you imparted upon me.'

'Then why do you bring this one before us?' the one on the left asked.

'To bring a mortal here without a proper offering is a great besmirchment' the one stooped up on the right side said. He swirled his goblet, which smelled of sour wine.

'He has courage,' she said, 'he crossed the river, while alive, out of curiosity. Should that not be rewarded?'

'We will tell him no more than what we told you,' the one on the left, who bobbed forward and backwards, said. He too had a drink that smelled yeasty.

'I agree,' said the one on the right. 'Not a word more.'

Both of the demons now spoke at the same time:

'At the dawn of your kind, the land was tilled and ploughed by men who knew nothing of the magic of bronze. They fought and did much evil, but then one of your ancestors caught the secret of bronze. He forged weapons that allowed him to slay and maim and lord over many others, and indeed, the tools crafted beat and cast and hunted so that your ancestors flourished, and more weapons could come into being. Next came the horse, of which man rode not just to plough the soil, but to bring him faster to his enemies. Soon came small roving bands of men armed with bronze, spreading pillage and rape and slaughter like disease, and all those who stood before them crumbled. Those were your ancestors, and they slew the giants that roamed the world, and routed the first men to oblivion. Next came he who harnessed iron, to change rock to metal, to smelt and forge and beat even deadlier weapons into the world, to sink into those weaker than they. From those small bands came kings, and dictators, and emperors, and they lord overall by cold, sharp, jinxed iron.

'This history, this truth, will be unknowable to your kind. Your bards and your druids and your priests could never fathom it. Your philosophers only touched upon one truth, like every piece of rock put to a touchstone until gold is yielded. Your philosophers called the earlier age an age of iron, where man was beholden to nothing except the search for glory, so that one's name may ring louder than the iron they slay with. That is all.'

I found nothing to say. Slighan nodded her head, then told the demons about Carthage, and Rome, and the massacres of Syracuse where thousands drowned, or of Cannae, where the earth drank so much blood that Dionysus would flush if he drank that much wine. She spoke of the comings and goings of famous men, generals or senators or warlords, and how their names ring like bells on cows. The two demons nodded along, until Slighan finished. She then placed the sprig of cypress at the squat feet of the two demons. Taking flint and iron from a pouch, she sparked a fire, and set the sprigs alight.

'I paid much for this,' she said, 'bestow your power upon me!'

'It is done,' the two demons said in unison.

'You see,' she said to me, 'this is my power. I have *the sight*, gifted by them. I can see into the Underworld, and bring it into ours. Now you know so much! My power will bring the world back into peace, before the times of bronze and iron and unbridled hatred! You have born witness to it!'

'You offer us much,' the two said in unison.

'Good demons,' I said, 'tell me what you wish for, and I will do it.'

A green light flickered across the eyes of the demon on the left, and then in the eyes of the one on the right.

'He offered us nothing,' said the one on the left.

'Nothing has been offered, you have blasphemed. Therefore, you will pay,' said the one on the right.

'You cannot be allowed to leave. You will stay here with us, and serve us here, in Hades.'

I gasped, my heart demanded I flee, yet my feet remained stubborn, and my shoes dug into the ground until hot sand poured between my toes.

'Please, good friends!' Slighan said and threw herself onto her knees. 'He paid the ferryman, he has the blessings of his god – allow him to leave with me!'

'It is decided,' the two said in unison. 'We shall have this man here, as a servant, to remind you to never bring a mortal without offering us great gifts.'

'No! I have given you so much,' Slighan cried, 'I pay the ferryman, who takes his toll on me – please, beloved friends, my dearest! Allow me to right this wrong!'

She cried while the demons sat silently. She turned to me, and grabbed a hold of me by my soiled robe. 'Why did you come here?!'

Slighan turned toward them once again and threw herself back on her knees. She whipped her head forward so that all of her hair fell in front of her, and she tore off her dress, her white naked body glowing against the dark-blue demons and their black divans.

'I beg you! I am at your mercy, oh great ones, tell me what you want!'

'No,' I said, and I pulled her to her feet. 'It was my transgression, do to me what is due. I will pay your toll,' I said to them, swallowing my words as their flickering green eyes seared through my courage, and I nearly loosened my bladder.

'No!' Slighan embraced me, but turned her head to the demons. 'Do what you will to me, and only me!'

'Then we will take a sacrifice from you,' said the one on the left.

'You will pay greatly,' said the one on the right.

'By the cold ground of Hades on which we stand – my soul to you – I grant it!'

'We will imbue you with the power to tear mortals asunder,' the one on the left said.

'On the island of Skye, you will reign as a queen, and bring sorrow to your enemies and allies alike.'

'You give me a gift?' she said, a look of bewilderment. 'There must be a catch!'

'We have spoken.'

She smiled. 'I know you not to be fools, but my eagerness remains bound. May we leave now, dear friends?'

'Leave, never return to our abode,' they said in unison. 'And know,' they said to me, 'that you too will pay a toll to us before you return to Hades.'

Her cold, soft hand grabbed mine, and we fled, leaving her dress flapping on the ground in the windless cavern.

Bring sorrow to your enemies and allies alike...

Chapter VII

When we left the cavemouth, the fog descended. Everything became blurry, and bleary, and just the white, nude, lithe form of Slighan showed me the way.

'One more place I must visit before we leave,' she said, 'it will be in haste! But we must, it is a necessity. Come, my dear friend.'

We raced across the cold sand in the mist, deep-blue gloom on all sides of us. After a while, a statue appeared in the mists. It was life-sized, a woman of serpentine stone, brandishing two hissing snakes in her clutches.

'O, goddess of mine, my patroness, of whom I am the last devotee,' she said, and prostrated before it, which I thought odd, for only men in the east did so for their gods.

Chin bumping against the sand, she spoke, 'I have nothing to offer, for I come before you skyclad, adrift, afraid. I left all my things at the feet of the demons of knowledge, who gave me the power to bring sorrow to my friends and enemies, and I know not now if I am gifted or hexed. Allow me to be the snake in your clutch, 'tis all I ask.'

She climbed to her feet as she snatched a piece of flint from the ground. 'You have revealed your wisdom to me,' she said. The edge of the sharp stone touched the blue veins of her wrist, and she bit her lip as she pressed down hard. Blood oozed out, and she held up her arm, trickles of blood sprinkling over her bare breasts and onto the red marble base of the statue, and a rivulet of ruby fell upon the sand.

Breathing heavily, she closed her eyes, her breasts heaved, her fists balled, and she lurched on the balls of her feet, then back to her heels. I edged closer to her, and then she stood akimbo before the statue.

A hissing sound eased out of one of the snakes held in the clutch of the statue. Then another hissing sound came from the other. The statue danced, swayed to and fro, and grinned a fanged smile. The white-painted eyes of the statue glowed fiery yellow. I grasped Slighan by her soft, bare shoulder.

'We must away,' I said, my voice but a murmur.

'No,' she said. Her pupils had become slits.

I smote her across the face. Her head flung backwards, her hair all astir, and when she pulled her head down, she hissed at me, two fangs dripping venom. I smote her again, she recoiled, and then snapped back toward me. She sank her teeth into my neck. I shrieked as the statue before us swayed, its arms bent like a dancer's as the snakes wriggled and whirled and snapped at the head of the goddess, which then cackled.

Blood trickled down my neck as Slighan slurped, but I grabbed a handful of her hair, closed my eyes, and headbutted her as hard as a smith beats iron. She crumpled as I caught her in my arms, and all became foggy.

When the fog had cleared, I opened my eyes, Slighan had been entangled with me, and we awoke in an empty, barren tomb. I still held my bleeding neck. Spoil heaps of loose dirt pocked in pottery sherds lay all around us. Slighan slid off of me as I untangled myself from her sweaty, oily body. She lay there in the dirt aloof as I found myself crawling between two sarcophagi, one with a lid ajar, the other agape and empty. The tunnel to leave the tomb was mounded in dirt. There were no figures in the chamber except faded, chipped painted walls. The room span round, and visions mired me: a ferryman, two blue-skinned demons, a demon holding two snakes, a woman holding a bundle of branches...

'I bit you,' she said, and laughed as she climbed to her feet, just as I found my head clearing up, and the visions faded.

'And I lost my dress,' she looked down at her nakedness. 'My Egyptian linen dress! And they accused us of bringing them cheap gifts!'

On my feet, I turned to free myself from this tomb.

'I bit you,' she said, licking the blood off her lips and feeling around on her forehead where a bruise blued. 'And you hit me!'

I said nothing in response.

'I could have you killed for that,' she said, and for a second, my darling daughter, a glint of red-yellow flashed in her eyes.

She took a breath, her frown vanished, and smiling now, she grabbed my hands.

'Yet death will not save you from what they will demand of you. There was nothing I could do, so I shall spare you the punishment.' Her red, hot, bloody lips kissed mine.

After a long spell, we left the tomb, much dirtier, sweatier, and bloodier than when we had entered, squeezing through the tall spoil heaps in the exit. Slighan stopped as she crawled, and turned to me.

'The cries and rings of battle! Something has transpired up there!'

'Let me go first then,' I said, and I scrambled around and then over her, and when the sunlight hit me, I squinted out.

Dozens of men fought among the mounds. Two lines had formed; one with Gauls and their knee-to-shoulder oblong shields and long thrusting spears, and one line brimmed with Slighan's men. Similar weaponry, but their shields painted black, and their hair without sheen in the sun. They all vied for victory over one another, thrusts of spears shot at the thighs of foemen, and on the flanks, youth duelled with short iron swords. A long iron thrusting spear with a flame-shaped blade thrust through the neck of one of Slighan's Gauls. One of Slighan's swordmen cleft down the head of a one-hand spearman, who crumbled to the ground, face mangled by the swordman's blade. Another of Slighan's Gauls, an old, wiry, greyed man shouted 'forward!' on the left flank.

Slighan crawled next to me, her mouth a smiling maw. 'Men fight for me. How uncouth would it be for me to appear naked before them! I must fetch my servants first!'

'Stay here,' I said, 'allow me to scout!'

'Nay! Scout?! Fight! Fight, brave fighter!' she said with a wink. 'Fight for your queen!'

As if I had just been born, I squeezed through the cramped entrance of the tomb to leave. I found myself amidst a battlefield. Iron-spear points vied for the flesh of men, as two dozen on each side lined up to fight, just nine paces from me. I had no idea if I had either friend or foe, and I looked around confused, much like a motherless lamb. Vericus rounded a mound and rushed to my side, his sword dangling from his waist.

'By the Gods, man, we thought you were lost forever – where have you been?'

'Nevermind, man,' I said, 'what is this?'

Three Gaulish youths rushed forward, their iron spears striking at their foes. One took a club to the knee, and then a spear jammed up into his groin. He bellowed, staggered forward through the enemy line, and collapsed at my side. His open mouth was against the dusty ground as he shivered in his death throes.

'The tribune is here for Slighan,' Vericus said. 'By Camulus! War comes!'

Before a decisive thought could come to me, a voice called from just beyond the mound.

'Ambicatos!'

I turned to see a familiar face, dressed in a cuirass of mail, a bronze visored helmet plumed with black horsehair, and one bronze greave on his left shin. He wielded a round shield painted with a boar, and a gladius. As he approached, his mail shimmered, the metal ruffling over his blood-red tunic.

'Antonius!' I said.

'She's down there, isn't she?' he asked, frowning, eyes ablaze. 'What has that witch done with you, that you vanish for three days?'

Three days?

'We have orders to execute her, for conspiring with deserters, for kidnapping a druid, for foul witchery, and who knows what else. By these old bones, I don the kit of Mars again because of that wretch. Move aside, my friend, and let me avenge whatever misdeeds she committed against you.'

I did not move.

'What, man? Can you not see the red field of Mars around you? What spell has she cast on you?'

'She saved me, my friend,' I said, 'I cannot budge.'

'You cannot tell me that! I have the authority of the consul, and I will enact their will. Step aside, I implore you – I beg you!'

'I will not,' I said, my knees buckling. 'What she did for me is indescribable.'

'You cannot fight a druid, our laws disallow that,' Vericus said, as he placed a sweaty hand on my dirty shoulder. 'My cousin, let me fight in your stead.' He put a hand to the antler-hilt of his sword in his scabbard.

Vericus and Antonius stood athwart one another, their eyes ready.

'Nay, Vericus,' I said to him, 'I speak the law, and I permit myself to fight. I was a warrior once. At ease, and I will fight my own battle.'

I seized the shield and spear of the dead Gaul at my feet, his cold grip on his spear was near-unrelenting. I kneeled before him, kissed him on the forward, and prayed to his shade to guide me to be as manly as he had been.

Antonius drew back, curled his shoulders, and cracked his neck. 'Old man,' he said, 'I am battle-hardened, well equipped, and I have a mission from above. Do not try me! You are bespelled by that witch, and I will kill you if I must, against my heart.'

'Kill me if you dare,' I said, and I adjusted the spearshaft in my hand. 'But I wish not to fight you, my friend. I owe Slighan my life, witch or not, spells or not, enchanted or not. Let us leave and you will not face the wrath of a man descended from Cuchulainn, the bravest of warriors.'

There was nothing more to say. We circled one another. The battlefield had been demarcated, a sward between the dead Gaul whose weapons I wielded, to the battleline of thrashing and thrusting warriors, to the mound of the demons' tomb where Slighan hid.

Antonius first raised his pilum, and I raised the spear in my hand.

'Ready?' he asked.

'Aye – go!' I shouted.

We cast our spears at one another. The pilum came for me, I raised my shield first, but I opted to sidestep out of the way. My javelin bounced off the edge of Antonius' shield. He knelt, grabbed it by the shaft off the ground, spun it around, and lobbed it, butt-end first at me. It landed at my feet.

'I knew when I first saw the fire in your eyes that we would settle this like men,' he said. He drew his gladius.

I knelt and drew the sword from the iron scabbard of the nameless, dead, young Gaul. I had his sword now, and it guided me, and I prayed to Lugus, god of all crafts, to guide my blade.

Antonius came scutum-first, and thrust his gladius at me. I sidestepped, leaning forward, remembering my footwork of right foot against the enemy, left foot behind. He mimicked me, took a sidestep and thrust at my thigh. I twisted my wrist to parry with the flat of the blade, flicked my wrist back and shoved his blade down, causing him to let go and allowing my blade to slide over his as he thrust it back up at my torso. I jumped back as he jumped forward, swatting his blade at my leg, and I pivoted, caught his blade against mine, and stabbed at him. He stepped back, and I gathered my feet and swiftly tilted forward, my iron sword stabbing him deep in the thigh under the skirt of his mail. He retched, and threw down his sword and shield.

Disarming the sword from him, I let my arms fall to the ground as I caught him. His cold, hard chainmail bristled against me as he breathed heavily. The blood poured from his wound.

'I bested you, in glorious single combat. Farewell, my dear friend,' I said to him, as he gasped, and stifled a whimper. I first leaned him back down to the ground, seized my discarded sword, and pointed it skyward. With a prayer to Lugus, I jammed the sword deep into his throat, and the blade pierced the skin like a knife to a soft cream. He gasped, gurgled, and spasmed. I raised the helmet off his head and put it aside, then I unbelted him, and pulling him up, lifted the chainmail off him. I unbuckled the single greave. I put the chainmail on overhead, and shimmied it onto my body; it rustled its way down. I belted myself with his swordbelt, and fitted his gladius into the scabbard. I strapped the greave to my right leg, and then helmeted myself, the horse-plume fluttering in the wind. I leaned down to the dead Gaul, hauled him on the shield I had taken, and placed the sword back into his belt. Facing westward, I prayed aloud to Lugus, thanking him for victory as I seized Antonius' scutum.

Slighan emerged from the tomb, dusty and dirty, unashamed of her nakedness as she clapped. 'My hero slew his beloved friend in my name! What a joyous day! Truly, I have been dignified as a queen.'

A shout, then men scrambled as the left flank of Slighan's men folded in a scurry and flurry of spears and slumping bodies. The line of Slighan's loyalists bowed, and a wedge of lime-haired Gauls broke through. Ash-haired Gauls lay dead and scattered, and three of them had been cornered against another mound, one bleeding. The iron-armed Gauls came with their spears toward us, five of them against me.

The spears were upon me. I raised Antonius' scutum as three spears jabbed at me, with three hits against the thick pinewood. Vericus leapt to my side, and he tossed a javelin. It impaled one of the enemies through the chest. I bent down, grabbed a javelin and so too tossed it, but a Gaul raised his shield as the javelin penetrated it. The Gaul then thrust his spear at me, I blocked, and then Vericus lunged forth, spear-first, and stabbed him in the groin. The enemy bounced backwards as I unsheathed the sword of Antonius. I lunged for their flank, slamming a spearshaft away with the edge of my shield, and with a hard step forward, slashed through the arm of a foe. My face spasmed as I prayed for the warp-spasm of Cuchulainn, hero of our clan, to boil within me, as the blood splashed over my face, and I thrust the gladius into the chest of a spear-wielding Gaul.

Vericus dropped his spear and drew his sword, and now we had both been upon the Gauls, and five of them lay shattered at our sandaled feet. We looked around, frantic, nervous for more foemen, but none came.

Slighan had now been clothed in a green wool dress, with her handmaidens crowded around her. Some of her surviving bodyguards had regrouped, one limping toward us. She climbed up on a low-lying mound, and she meant to rouse us, but a horn blew in the distance. More foemen came trudging up the high hill, and there the Etruscan priest, upon a hillock, waved them on and pointed at us.

'We must flee!' I said, and I ran toward Slighan as I sheathed Antonious' sword, wrapped my arms around her waist, and hoisted her up. She held onto my neck as we started down the slope of the hill straight away. We came down the hill and forded a stream, with the stragglers of Gauls and handmaidens behind us.

'You killed in my name, mighty warrior,' Slighan said, her voice low in my ear.

We ran hard through the forest, and headed towards a dock at the river. Slighan led us to some small boats, and piling in, we paddled downriver until nightfall.

After traversing into a dell, a deep pocket of forest nestled somewhere in the Apennines, we found a cave, high away from the shepherd's trail we had taken. Sheep fled from the cavemouth as we entered it, and we set up camp.

The cave had been littered with human bones, undoubtedly from bandits and suchlike. After a rest, Slighan's Gauls squatted around the campfire as the sky darkened, feeling much like savages. I took off my armour and weapons and squatted in just a mere loincloth around the campfire with Vericus, listening to the wolves howling in the distance during twilight. Slighan's handmaidens were busybodied with some water from the stream while some foraged berries. Two handmaidens sat around the fire, each banging a round rock against a piece of grey flint, cracking chips off the flint. They sat there knapping, likely arrowheads, and I could almost hear that iron-voiced demon ring within me with each crack of the hammerstone.

'You old dog you – you have some fight left,' Vericus said with a grin. 'You ought to be a warrior again.'

'I never thought I would fight again, yet the warp-spasm flashed in me,' I said with a sigh. 'I would much rather learn more of the stars.'

'Will be hard to do so in Italia. You're an outlaw now.'

'So are you,' I said. 'We will head for our home islands now, of Skye and Eigg, because that is where the queen believes she should go. We must visit your father on Eigg, and then I can depart for Skye.'

'Eigg calls me,' he said, 'if that is what has been spun for me. We'll see what my father thinks of this Slighan, and what she can offer our clan.'

We sat there, side by side, the sunless dell and its endless dark trees before us. A handmaiden cooed behind us, and handed us each a small wool pouch.

'Your share of the spoils,' she said.

Opening the pouches, we found a handful of silver coins, with the bust of Artemis on the obverse, and a lion on the reverse.

'Coins without an oath,' he said. 'Is this fitting for a sacrifice to the gods of this cave?'

I looked back at the bleakness, with a single light dancing from the bend where Slighan had her quarters. Sliding the coins into my hand, I chucked them out of the cavemouth, and they scattered all over the slope and down into the unknown outside.

'For Antonius Nero, fearsome warrior and good tribune,' I said.

Vericus, leaving the cinch of the pouch open, tossed it over his shoulder and deep into the cave. The coins rang throughout the cave.

'For my oathless life,' he said, 'good riddance to it. I return to my father and serve him as his retainer on Eigg. Let the gods drape him with the right oath, to serve Slighan or not.'

Leaving my cousin at the cavemouth, I retired deeper in the cave, where Slighan's handmaidens had laid out a makeshift bedroom, with a wide wool blanket to mark the room, and a bed of some heather and moss. Slighan's red-nailed hand beckoned me in, where a single candle had been lit, and one of her handmaidens sat, rubbing olive oil over her bare back. When satisfied, she shooed the maiden aside, and pulled me into her bed. She spoke softly to me.

'That tribune you slew was your friend.'

'My dearest,' I said.

'What theatrics!' she said with a grin. 'Why, your heart must mourn for him.'

'It does.'

'There is little time to mourn when we are on the move! Gaze upon me,' she said, her sticky body gleaming in the candlelight, 'what sort of immoralities would be heaped upon me, to live as an outlaw, hunted by stuffy men who care only for their own personal glories or to fatten their coin purses? Onward to amass my army, so the First Men may walk on Gaia again!

'Your cousin, the warrior Vericus – he shall bestow men upon me?'

'He could bestow many,' I said, 'he is the son of the chief of Eigg.'

'A plan forms,' she said. 'We will venture to Eigg, and win over the Britons there! Soon thereafter, Skye will be my throne. I shall have legions, rivalled only by those of Rome and Carthage and Macedon and Persia. None shall doubt my queenship then.'

Badb, the goddess of fear, seemed to creep in my throat. Slighan reclined on her litter of pillows upon a herringbone-spun yellow blanket over the hard-dirt, sheep-dung floor of the cave. She eyed me, grinning, sipping wine from a silver goblet. 'What say you, Ambicatos, druid of Skye? What say you that I shall reign over Skye, as a sovereign, decreed by the blue demons of the Underworld?'

'I think you will run into a lot of haughty Britons,' I said.

'Then let them be as haughty as boars! They do not know what I know – nay – what we know, what has been decreed by the Underworld itself.'

She grabbed me by the collar of my formerly white tunic, stained black in blood, dirt, and grease from Antonious' chainmail, and pulled me close to her. Her silky black hair groomed, her linen-clung body bathed, her hot breath on my neck, the smoothness of her body enticed me, as the scent of lavender danced in my nostrils.

And there, in her bedchambers, I spent another night.

Chapter VIII

In the morning, we assembled in boats along the river. Carrying the armour, shield, and sword of Antonius, I stood over the rocky-shored river. I cast the bronze helmet in first; the horse-plume floated upon the surface before it, too, sank with the helmet. With both of my hands, I sent the chainmail flying high before it vanished below the murky water as fast as a shooting star. I flung the shield which whirled through the air before its edge scraped the surface and rode the wave. Finally, the single bronze greave hit the current which pulled it for a span before it sank.

'Antonius Nero, tribune and Roman, and friend,' I said, 'I sacrifice your belongings to Lugus, who granted me victory. May your shade find rest, and may you be reborn in three generations, a as a warrior to walk Taman again.' With a kiss to the flat of the blade, his gladius slunk down into the depths of the river. There, at the riverbank, I pondered on the loss of my dear, dead friend, until a deep caw echoed from further up the valley. A raven flew downriver, past me and into the green gloom of the treed mountains. From a glance toward the sun, I figured it flew southward. Shuddering, I headed back to the cave, the visages of the blue demons alive in my mind.

Under the cover of war, we fled Italia. In Massalia, we spent the summer on the outskirts of the city, in the little vineyards and coves along the coast. Slighan and her men often ventured forth to the city, and always returned with more men, or the promises of more men; mostly deserters of the war ravaging Italia. Soon came not only Gauls, but Romans from a range of provinces, Etruscans, Sicilians, Samnites, Carthaginians, Iberians, Macedonians, Greeks from Neapolis and elsewhere, and her numbers swelled like the tide on a full moon. The northern wind hit Massalia hard, and taking it as an omen, we set sail back for the Hebrides, up the Rhone and to the Atlantic.

All along the river, we travelled with amphorae of wine and olive oil, crates of figs, fine linen and even silk. Slighan's Gaulish chiefs traded with local Gaulish chiefs upriver, and many swore allegiance to her. Our party reached the Atlantic, we sailed up to Albion, and back to the Hebrides, close to my home island of Skye.

We landed on Eigg where our clan Ashaig had a stronghold, and, were received well by the druids there; we rested at the harbour.

Slaves ploughed in the fields around the harbour, which lay in the shadow of a rocky, high mountain centred on the small island. The mountain had been crowned in drystone walling stuffed between tors and rises and impasses, forging the fortress of Dun Sgùrr. The chief Auscetes dwelled up there – the father of Vericus, and my uncle.

We headed up to announce our arrival, trudging the well-beaten path. Slighan stepped heavily, and heaved; strange to me, since she could dance up such a mountain without so much as a fast heartbeat in the dance's wake. Her handmaidens aided her up the slope but she once lost her footing on scree, slid, and nearly stumbled back down. Two young Gauls hauled her up on their shoulders. When we met the man-high stone walls guarded by spear-wielding, gruff-looking men in salmon-coloured cloaks, we knew we had reached the summit of my uncle's fort.

The wind blew heavily on the peak; there a massive round hall stood, with a stone-lined foundation, waddle-daub walls, and a thatched roof with a billow of smoke stretching upward. The spear-wielding Gauls, nine of them, cheered and aimed their spears skyward, shouting the name of Epona, the goddess of travellers, for a safe return of the chief's son.

Vericus and I, followed by Slighan with three of her handmaidens and nine of her now black-haired chiefs, arrived at the courtyard of the hall. She had with her Gaulish chiefs from the Liguri, the Helveti, the Veneti, the Boii, Tartessians from Iberia, a Samnite, and a Numidian. A druid in a pure white robe met us outside the flower-adorned garden of the chief's hall.

'Where is my father?' Vericus asked, 'he should see me with such a retinue!'

The Eigg-men all turned grim. The druid turned to Vericus, crestfallen.

'We reckoned to tell you once you reached his summit, under endless blue Nemos, and above your island and the seas, on the roof of Taman, that Auscetes was taken by illness two weeks ago today. He watches from the far west, with pride, as you parade up the mountain to return home, with such richly dressed foreigners, and your druid cousin of Skye.'

Vericus turned his head aside, seized his spear, and tossed it heavenward. We never saw it come down.

'And that makes you chief!' Slighan said to Vericus, and wrapped an arm around him. 'Show me your hall, great chief of Eigg!'

Vericus looked among our clansmen, who had their heads bowed.

'Raise your heads, raise your spears, raise your spirits,' he said. 'We drink to my father's memory.'

The hall was nine-men high, nine-horses wide, and round, as is the custom of our houses in Albu. It was decked in shields and spears every nine paces, and the hearth, tended by clan slaves, broiled a soup in an iron cauldron set hanging from two iron firedogs, the ends of which were forged into the shape of shrieking boars. The warriors were seated around the roundtable, while myself and Slighan were seated at a separate table. She had brought our clan gifts of grapes, wine, and olive oil, and all three had been divided between the tables and benches in the hall.

Auscetes' body had been laid out on a litter and dressed in his war gear, with his shoes on the wrong feet and with wine, beer, and boar all laid out around him. We danced, drank, and sang around his body in the smoky hall.

After the feast, nine warriors, including Vericus, brought my uncle's body out of the hall, to the outside, and laid him upon a wooden platform, crows cawing in the distance. Morrigan, goddess of death, would send her children, the crows, the magpies, the ravens, to have their feast as well, to send off the earthly remains back to the Otherworld. Vericus sat there and waited all night, silent and without food or drink or sleep, as the children of the Morrigan bowed their black heads over my uncle.

That night we tented around the hall, and Slighan, who had not slept with me in a month, barged into my tent. Wearing a silk shawl, she beckoned my attention, and with a foot upon a stool, she unclasped the shawl and revealed her swollen belly.

'I am with child, my dear druid,' she said with a smile. 'The bag of wheat burst, so it is a girl. A girl, brought into this iron-cold world.'

I stood wordless.

'You have planted your seed in me,' she said with a half-smile, 'it grows. We have a princess, for I am queen.' She clasped her shawl, and her eyes widened. 'I desire no king. Whatever will we do, my darling druid? For if I were to marry, it needs to be beneficial. I deserve nothing less.'

'And I am betrothed to another,' I said, with a sigh.

She walked widdershins around the tent. 'Whatever will we do, my darling druid? This baby causes me to spew, to stumble, and will soon scratch in my belly. Yet my love swells, as my belly does – a princess,' she stopped and cradled herself. 'If I were to declare that this baby came to me through the love of a centaur or a giant or a god – I would be believed, for I have the power of *the sight*, and your clansmen will kneel before it. But I desire not that! I will keep this child secret, and when she is born, I will simply have my handmaidens raise her. Nay, my Banaghaisgeich!'

Banaghaisgeich, our word for Amazons.

'Your Banaghaisgeich? But they are just a legend,' I said.

'Perhaps they are, Ambicatos. Perhaps they aren't. Perchance they won't remain such.'

After a spell, she spoke. 'And you, Ambicatos, do you not miss your betrothed? Twenty years you have spent on Mona, and now nearly half a year among my ranks – you must be boiling with longing for her! Return to her, and leave your Armenian lover among her warriors. I will not begrudge you for it. I will be just fine.'

She tossed her hair over her shoulder, and with a wink, she left my tent. She poked her head back in. 'Return in eight months, and you may witness the birth of your daughter. But silence! Beware the wrath I shall bring upon you if you ever dare crow about what transpired back in the tomb of the two blue demons!'

At dawn, I met Vericus, and we embraced, and he lent me a little boat and a paddle. I paddled back over to Skye alone, to return after twenty years to Dun Ashaig. I was to be initiated into the druid order there, and finally wed my betrothed, Aine.

Chapter IX

Eighteen months later, a woman came to Dun Ashaig with a message for me. She wore tall leather boots, with a red tunic, and was cowled in a brown hood. She had paddled over to the harbour on a small boat, and when I got into the boat with her, I found a bow, strung taut, with a quiver of a dozen goose-feather fletched arrows. I found it odd, but odder still was the sight southward on Eigg, when we arrived there.

Dozens of bow-armed women guarded the harbour when we arrived. My ferrywoman and some of the bowwomen there at the harbour exchanged words in a tongue I did not understand, and then she escorted me toward Dun Sgùrr. When the clouds parted and the sun hit her face, I knew her as the eldest of Slighan's handmaidens.

Twilight apexed, the overcast sky in the early spring daunted me as we scrambled up the steep hills to the fort. A grim-faced Vericus greeted me at the entrance, among throngs of Gauls, and he waved me in.

'The Queen will see you, not him,' my escort said.

'Forget her,' Vericus said, 'cousin, it has been months, and there is much to discuss with you!'

'Nay,' the escort said, as she strung an arrow into her bow and aimed the flint-tipped head at Vericus. 'The Queen's will must not be disobeyed.'

With a retch, I turned to Vericus, who looked forlorn. 'This is how it's been since you left,' he said. 'And tomorrow is when I shall swear my men to her.'

I started in the direction ordered by the bowwoman, my eyes still meeting Vericus'. We headed toward the edge of the plateau, so close to the side that I worried about tumbling down the cliff, and the bowwoman pulled me down into an alcove. There, some canvas had been set up, guarded by two more bowwomen, and they led me inside.

There Slighan was reclining on a bed, arms crossed, in a long brown dress. A baby cooed and whined, bundled up and cradled by a blond wet nurse. I sat next to Slighan, and she laid her head in my lap. The wet nurse passed the baby to me, and I held my daughter for a long while.

Trumpets woke me in the morning, cuddled next to Slighan. Her bowwomen hectored me out, and after I had readied myself, we all met at the hall. We ate the last of the grapes, and drank the rest of the wine, so much so that some of Vericus' men slumped on their chairs, or staggered around the hall.

At midday, the trumpeters sounded again. Slighan came bedecked in her silk shawl, with a girdle of woad-dyed linen. Flanked by her bowwomen, she stood upon a dais, and called for a moot. Chiefs from the surrounding islands joined with their men, and they all unarmed themselves at the area marked by holly boughs. One by one, they went up to the dais, knelt, and kissed Slighan's hand. They then stood aside, in throngs, as the handmaidens danced around them, rattling their rattles, and beating their drums.

After all of the former warriors had sworn their oaths to Slighan, Vericus began to approach her. At the midway of his approach, Slighan pointed to a leather scabbard that hung at his side under his cloak. He drew it back to show a sword in his scabbard.

'You come to me armed – shall you jinx our oath?' she asked.

'My father always went to the moot armed,' he said as he drew to a stop. All looked at him.

'I have no concern whether you are armed or unarmed, for the goddess herself, Hecate, defends me like aegis defends Minerva. What have you – have you not the word, that your sword must be surrendered to me? Have you known that henceforth all iron shall be forbidden for you?'

Vericus turned his head toward the bare platform where the bones of his father had fallen off. He looked back and stared Slighan down.

'Surrender my iron?' he said and sneered, then he spat. 'I will have you know that Vercerterx himself trained me in the arts of swordsmanship! My sword will never be separated from me, until the shoes are put on my wrong feet, and I am hoisted out of Taman in battle.'

All stood silent. Only the crackling of the campfire came and croaks of seagulls in the distance sounded.

'The courage of this man! Why, I ought to commend you, come forward, and leave that sharpened rod of iron at your side!' she said as she threw her hands up.

Vericus approached her. He was nearly a head taller than her. She raised her sceptre.

'All I ask is that you may stoop down so I may bless you, and have your oath, swordsman, trained by Vercerterx, son of Auscetes, cousin to druid Ambicatos, and chief of Eigg.'

He leaned forward. She gripped the sceptre with both hands, and in a slow, heavy arc, she slammed the sceptre across his forehead. He crumbled to the ground on his back, his arms shot out skyward.

Commotion ripped across the throngs of men, the women stilled their instruments, and Slighan stood heaving over the fallen Vericus.

'Let it be known that besmirchment is punishable! I am the queen of the First Men! War I bring!'

She shot a glance to a handful of the warriors who retreated, and vaulted over the waist-high walls one by one, undoubtedly fetching their iron. I fell by my cousin, who drooled, and nothing more, and I reckoned to slay him, for no warrior should linger so long, sullied by a cheap strike.

Slighan's faithful beelined for the tents around the hall, and many weaved into the tents unarmed, and then weaved out armed, with long iron-bladed spearheads, clubs, or some crudely-made flint-headed axes. They funnelled out to meet their enemies, Vericus' brothers-in-arms that returned, iron glinting in the sun, on the other side of the wall.

Spears thrust over the wall, scraping the drystone from both ends of it. One of Slighan's spearmen sank his weapon into the belly of a foe, ripped his spear out, and the foe's guts spilt out with it. One of Vericus' men, shouting the name of his lord, leapt onto the wall and tossed a club.

The club bounced off the head of a foe, who fell flat, but the club-thrower took a spear to the groin. Another retainer of Vericus crumbled over the wall and with a spearshaft, broken, impaling him through the back, while another retainer retched as a stone-headed axe bit into his chest in a chasm of blood. All the while, Slighan, on her dais, raised her sceptre into the air and cried out the name of Hecate, as her bone-rattlers, drummers, and flute-players all pranced about her like happy fawns.

The bowwomen, nine of them, climbed up on a broad rock outcrop, notched their bowstrings with their grey-feather arrows, traced their sights on the warriors streaming up the escarpment toward the walls, and one spearman fell over, sighing.

A retainer of Vericus', armed with a flame-tongued spear, leapt over the rampart and onto the sward, hopped over a dying axman, and rushed towards the formation of bowwomen. He stabbed at the women, and one bowwoman hopped down as he stabbed another through the side. The spearman retracted his spear from the slain woman, then shoved it into the groin of another, who slumped over the shaft in a mess of blood and vomit. Soon the women shouted, and one by one, began to hop off of the outcrop. Some of Slighan's loyalists had rebelled, and nine of them – armed with spears and clubs – ran over toward me. I scuttled out of the way. One grey-haired, fury-faced Gaul ran toward my dead cousin, bent over, and unsheathed his sword out of his scabbard, and charged the dais. I recognized him now as Divico – the old friend of my cousin we met at the crossroads in Etruria.

Slighan's dancers scrambled out of the way as the rebels screamed *Vericus* as loud as they could, rampaging across the sward. Two in the rear chucked javelins that pierced through the headwind and into the bodies of two of Slighan's bodyguards, who came armed with stone-headed axes, and two more of her men behind the axe-men crumbling to the ground readied slings. Slingshots snapped through the air and two of the rebels fell; their comrades leapt over their bodies and into the fray.

Divico evaded a slash from an axe of one of Slighan's bodyguards. The old Gaul parried a spear thrust, then knocked another spear out of the way with his shield, and raced toward both foemen. Divico slashed an arm off the first spearman, then sliced cleanly through the shoulder of the other and kept running through them. One jump and he came upon the dais, sword raised, the red fire of Camulus, god of war, in his eyes.

Slighan's mouth parted as a volley of arrows rained down at her attacker. Divico flung up his oblong shield and knelt under it, the arrows pelted around him and the shield. The queen pivoted as he leapt up like a salmon at her, sword drawn and poised for her soft, white, supple, unarmoured body. She turned to her bodyguards. Three paces from her, all of her bodyguards had been piled in a heap of dead and wounded, and the rebels closed in on her, black-bloodied spears first.

Fire all over. A spew of it, like seafoam, of pure, hot, red-yellow flames. It engulfed Divico as he hid behind his shield. Sulphur assaulted my nostrils, I gagged on the smoke, the roar of flame overcame me, and as if my face had been put near a boiling cauldron, sweat trickled down my face. It was real, hot fire, yet when it stopped, Divico did not lay burned. He stood, awestruck, and then he fell, pecked by so many arrows like the pricks of a hedgehog.

Slighan now turned to the rebels, who stood stupefied. Some of them had dropped their weapons. One young spearman held his weapon flaccid in his hands, mouth agape. I now saw it, my dear daughter. A flash of it, a quickening pulse, like the onset of a dream before being abruptly awakened. A gargantuan, red, reptilian body sprawled out over the dais. A long, red, scaly neck. Two wings that spanned like the wings of ninety eagles combined. A face remained lizardlike, but still a woman's, with red-yellow eyes. It screeched.

Three of the rebels ran, dashing toward the far end of the plateau. They attempted to scale down the walls. Another had fallen to his knees and crawled away. The final stood there, just staring, and he did not budge until Slighan – now herself again – stood before him with the raised stone sceptre. He raised his hands but the heavy macehead crashed through his defence and smashed his face in.

I rolled up to my feet and I raced toward the hall. What I had seen, I could not fathom. She had shown me the Underworld, and I had conversed with the two blue demons, and grovelled before the snake-woman, and even endured Slighan sucking my blood. Yet, when she had, her eyes had glowed in the colours that they had when that dragon – yes – dragon, flared up before me and Vericus' retainers. Whatever she was, or whatever happened, I cared not to allow my daughter to be reared by that. I rushed down to the alcove, ripped aside the canvas, shoved away the midwife, smote the wetnurse who fell backwards, and then seized my daughter while she sucked at the falling wetnurse's breast. I seized a sling from a table, bundled my daughter up in it, and headed out post-haste.

Back outside, Vericus' retainers had taken the wall. They spilt over it, like a flooded river, but the bowwomen regained their vantage point, and loosened more arrows upon them like a startled porcupine releasing its quills. I could see no way down, for the entrance had been crowded in fighters and death.

All over the sward, Slighan's men scrambled into a formation like the five-marked side of a Roman die. Led by young gladius-wielding Samnites, they marched toward Vericus' remaining Gauls. I headed the opposite way, seaward, toward the cliffsides where some of the fleeing men, as I had now seen, lay battered like broken beetles several spans below.

I slung my daughter over my shoulder, on my back, and with a prayer to Good Danu, the mother goddess of all, I clambered down the cliff. Foot by foot, edge by edge, earth crumbling beneath my feet, I went down the cliffside, all the while the clangs of iron rang above, and the wind carried the stench of blood. My daughter began to wail hard.

As I descended the cliffside, nearly midway, a figure emerged on the edge of the cliff. I peered and saw Slighan, just a silhouette against the now rising sun. She looked down at me, and she shouted: 'Return my daughter to me at once, Ambicatos!'

I said nothing in response. I continued my descent, now finding sure-footed placings until I ended up on even ground. Seaward now, I headed toward the harbour. Funnelling down from the mountain, a great army came, dozens of men racing forth. Among them, glowing in her shimmering white-silver dress, came Slighan. I blinked, and for a brief moment, there behind her army, the two wings of a dragon beat.

At the harbour, two bronze-skinned fishermen with buckets of silvery fish and some nets had just beached at the jetty. I pulled a bunch of my soiled, torn, white robe up at my collar, and with my other hand, I gestured toward my vestments.

'I am the druid Ambicatos of Clan Ashaig – I demand passage to Skye!'

'Aye,' said one fisherman, as he looked over my shoulder at the armour racing down. The three of us pushed the boat over the sand and shells and into the lapping tide. Ankle-deep, the boat began to float and the two of them hopped in. I unslung my daughter and held her to my breast as I stepped in.

'They have bowmen,' said one of the fishermen.

'They will not fire upon us as long as I have her – just paddle!'

They paddled, the little wicker boat caught the tide, and we began to drift toward the nearest wing of Skye, its most southerly headland, the breeze flowing through my hair, and my daughter crying her brown eyes out.

On the beach, Slighan's men all hunched up together, and then broke to make a gangway. Slighan stomped both of her feet as she walked through the sand toward the sea, hiked up her dress, and stopped knee-deep in the water. Her bowwomen aimed their bows, her slingers their slingshots, her spearmen their javelins, but nothing was fired or slung or cast at us. I ran my fingers over the black baby hair of my daughter.

'Druid Ambicatos! I hex you!' she shouted downwind, as the tide swelled around her ankles. 'Ruination will be brought upon your clan like lions upon deer! Death, destruction, decimation – all shall follow! Beware the hag of the hills – for I will don her red robe, and I will beat my wings upon your island of Skye! On the island of Skye, I will reign as a queen, and bring sorrow to your enemies and allies alike!

'My army of First Men will annihilate Clan Ashaiger, your wife will be befouled by the most well-endowed donkey, and your body forgotten in the foulest-smelling bog. Know your foulness, for you will witness this all as your soul will be drunk in shame in the Underworld! Abhorred druid! I will bide my time, and await to return to Skye with an even bolder, more violent, more brutal army, and we will subsume Skye and I shall reign over as queen with my daughter at my side!'

The fishermen paddled; one with heavy breaths. The other put a hand on my shoulder as I held my baby closer to my chest.

'I hex you!' Slighan shouted as the wind changed and blew her black hair all askew. 'I hex you!' she mouthed upwind.

As our boat headed into the sound, Slighan and her men all stood on the beach in silence. I shuddered as they sank over the horizon, while the currents rocked our vessel. We headed landward, then hugged the coast, and they paddled all afternoon.

At sunset, we arrived at the quiet harbour of Ashaig. I ambled out of the boat, my daughter clinging to my chest. I sat upon a hillock, wiped snot from my daughter's nose with my sleeve, the sun behind her. She cooed and giggled. Pondering what to tell my beloved Aine, I headed for the nearest farm for comfort and aid. I hatched a story around the hearthfire that she was a foundling, an illegitimate child of a dear friend that I had sworn to raise, and named her Myrnna, after my grandmother.

Thus, we raised you, Myrnna, my daughter, and kept the truth of your parentage, and this history, from you for sixteen years until now, on the eve of the end of our clan. I entrust you now to a crafty warrior, Brennus, who will protect you and bring you to the sanctuary of Dun

Torrin. I now meet my end, to witness the annihilation of my clan, and to enter shame as I sink into the Underworld, the fulfilled hex of Slighan.

Epilogue

No, my dear daughter. I fight. I will dispel the hex of Slighan – I will be crowned king of the Ashaigers, and I shall walk like a warrior once more, and shall sing the song of spear and sword and vie against the Hillmen, Slighan's hordes, to show that so-called queen that I am still that fighter I once was in my youth, hoary and tired as I am.

The fate of our clan is certain, but my fate in the Underworld, and what the blue demons shall bestow upon me, remains unknown to me. I will leave that for the druids of this world to ponder. For now, I drink, and tomorrow, I battle, and at twilight, I die. The warp-spasm will boil within me once more before I pay the toll to Hades.

Goodnight, Myrnna.

On the island of Skye, you will reign as a queen, and bring sorrow to your enemies and allies alike.

Did you love *Tomb of the Blue Demons*? Then you should read *Hag of the Hills* by JTT Ryder!

"Nothing is unconquerable; even our gods can die."Brennus is destined from birth to become a warrior, despite his farmer's life. But when the Hillmen kill his family and annihilate his clan, he now has the opportunity to avenge those who he loved.Brennus must survive endless hordes of invading Hillmen and magic-wielding sidhe, aided by only a band of shifty mercenaries, and an ancient bronze sword.Failure means his family and clan go unavenged. Victory will bring glory to Brennus and his ancestors.Hag of the Hills is a heroic fantasy novel set in 200 B.C. on the Isle of Skye, steeped in Celtic mythology and culture.

Read more at www.oldworldheroism.com.

Also by JTT Ryder

The Bronze Sword Cycles
Tomb of the Blue Demons
Hag of the Hills
The Lion of Skye

Watch for more at www.oldworldheroism.com.

About the Author

Joseph Thomas Thor Ryder is an archaeologist and author of the heroic fantasy novel Hag of the Hills, book 1 of The Bronze Sword Cycles duology. He is a published author of Viking archaeology, and a doctoral candidate specializing in the Viking Age and Celtic Iron Age. He resides in Norway where he conducts archaeological research and writes heroic fantasy set in historical periods.

Read more at www.oldworldheroism.com.

www.ingramcontent.com/pod-product-compliance
Lightning Source LLC
Chambersburg PA
CBHW051353150726
48000CB00003B/1173